One Watermelon Seed

Celia Barker Lottridge

illustrations by Karen Patkau

Fitzhenry & Whiteside

Text copyright © 2008 by Celia Barker Lottridge
Illustrations copyright © 2008 by Karen Patkau

Originally published in 1986 by Oxford University Press
First published by Fitzhenry & Whiteside in 2008

Published in Canada by Fitzhenry & Whiteside, 195 Allstate Parkway, Markham, Ontario L3R 4T8

Published in the United States by Fitzhenry & Whiteside, 311 Washington Street, Brighton, Massachusetts 02135

www.fitzhenry.ca   godwit@fitzhenry.ca

10 9 8 7 6 5 4 3

Library and Archives Canada Cataloguing in Publication
Lottridge, Celia B. (Celia Barker)
One watermelon seed / Celia Barker Lottridge ; illustrated by Karen Patkau.
ISBN 978-1-55455-034-0
1. Counting—Juvenile literature.   2. Gardening—Juvenile literature.
I. Patkau, Karen II. Title.
QA113.L67 2008   j513.2'11   C2007-907004-3

U.S. Publisher Cataloging-in-Publication Data
(Library of Congress Standards)
Lottridge, Celia B. (Celia Barker).
One watermelon seed / Celia Barker Lottridge ; illustrated by Karen Patkau.
Originally published: Toronto, ON: Oxford Univ Press, 1986.
[32] p. : col. ill. ; cm.
Summary: Max and Josephine plant their garden, where there are ample opportunities
to count by ones. And when the crops are harvested, it's time to count by tens.
ISBN: 978-1-55455-034-0
1. Counting — Juvenile literature.   2. Gardening — Juvenile literature.   I. Patkau, Karen.   II. Title.
513.211 [E] dc22   QA113.L688 2008

Fitzhenry & Whiteside acknowledges with thanks the Canada Council for the Arts, and the Ontario Arts Council
for their support of our publishing program. We acknowledge the financial support of the Government of Canada
through the Book Publishing Industry Development Program (BPIDP) for our publishing activities.

Design by Wycliffe Smith Designs

Printed in Hong Kong, China

For Anna Louise
— CBL

To Noire and Koko, who were there
from the beginning
— KP

Max and Josephine planted a garden.

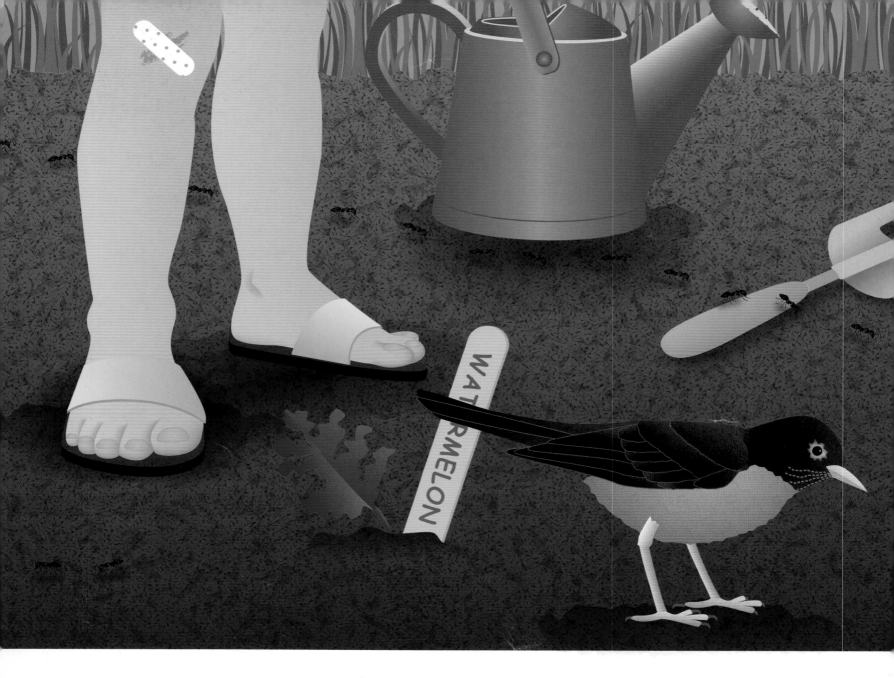

They planted one watermelon seed...and it grew.

1

They planted two pumpkin seeds...and they grew.

1 2

Max planted three eggplants...and they grew.

1 2 **3**

Josephine planted four pepper seeds...and they grew.

1 2 3 4

Then she planted five tomato plants...and they grew.

1 2 **3** 4 5

Max planted six blueberry bushes...and they grew,

1 2 **3** 4 5 **6**

and seven strawberry plants...and they grew.

1 2 **3** 4 5 6 7

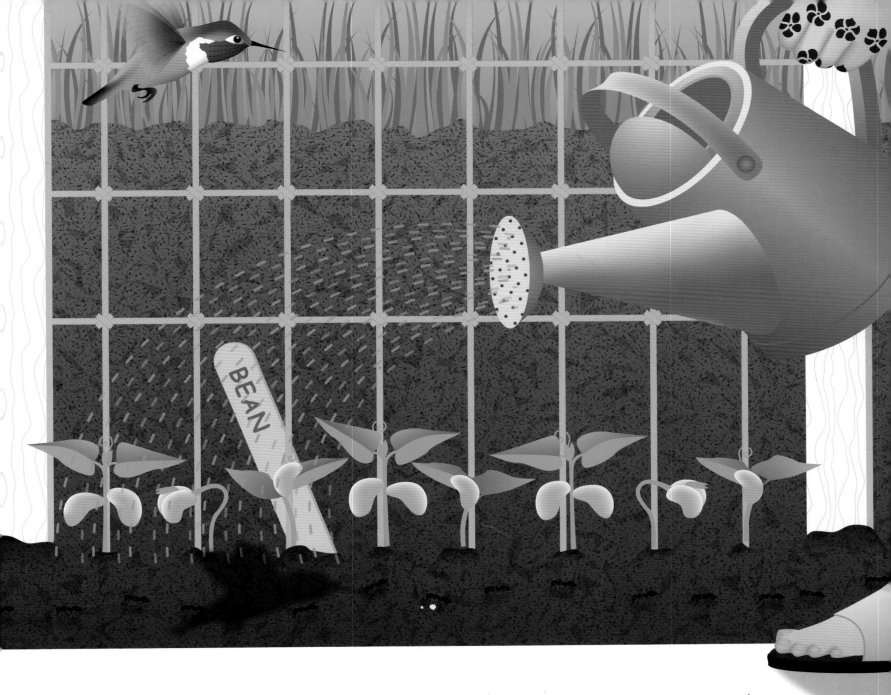

Josephine planted eight bean seeds...and they grew,

1 2 **3** 4 5 **6** 7 **8**

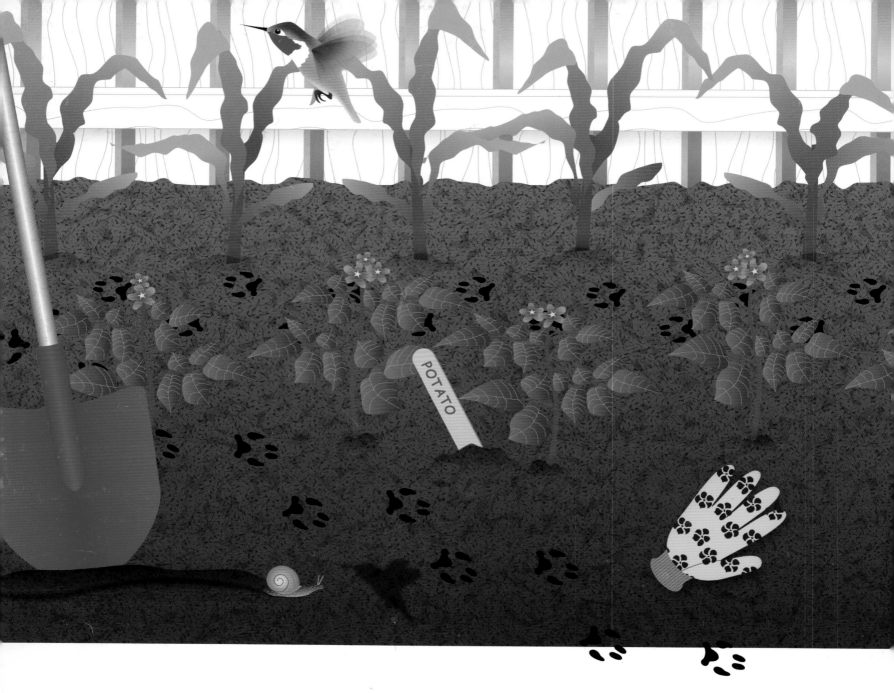

and nine seed potatoes...and they grew.

1 2 3 4 5 6 7 8 9

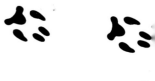

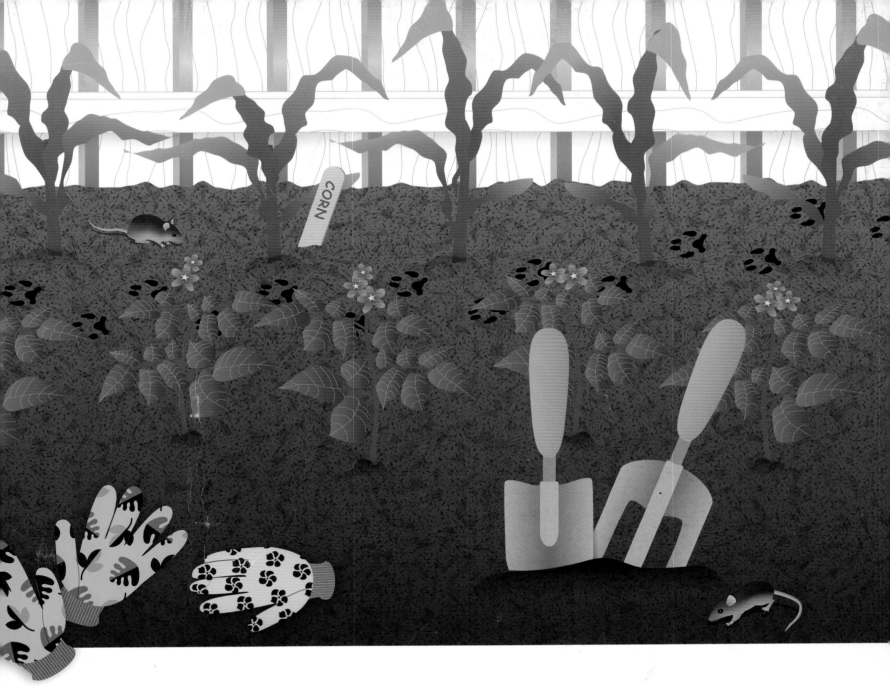

They planted ten corn seeds...and they grew.

1 2 **3** 4 5 **6** 7 **8** 9 10

The rain fell and the sun shone. The seeds and the leaves, the stalks and the vines **grew** and **grew** and **grew**.

Max and Josephine weeded and watered and waited.

One day they looked at their garden and saw

there was plenty to pick. So...

They picked ten watermelons, big and green,

and twenty pumpkins, glowing orange.

10 20

Max picked thirty eggplants, dark and purple,

10 20 30

and forty peppers, shiny yellow.
10 20 **30** 40

They both picked fifty tomatoes, plump and juicy,

10 20 **30** 40 50

and sixty blueberries, small and round.

10 20 **30** 40 50 **60**

Josephine picked seventy strawberries, sweet and red.

10 20 **30** 40 50 **60** 70

Max picked eighty string beans, thin and crisp.

10 20 **30** 40 50 **60** 70 80

Josephine dug ninety potatoes, nobby and brown,

10 20 **30** 40 50 **60** 70 **80** 90

and they picked one hundred ears of corn.

10 20 **30** 40 50 **60** 70 **80** 90 100

It was not ordinary corn. Max and Josephine saved it
for cold winter nights, when the garden was
covered with snow.

Then they turned it into 100s and 1000s of big, white crunchy puffs because that corn was

POPCORN

Look inside the garden fruits and vegetables.

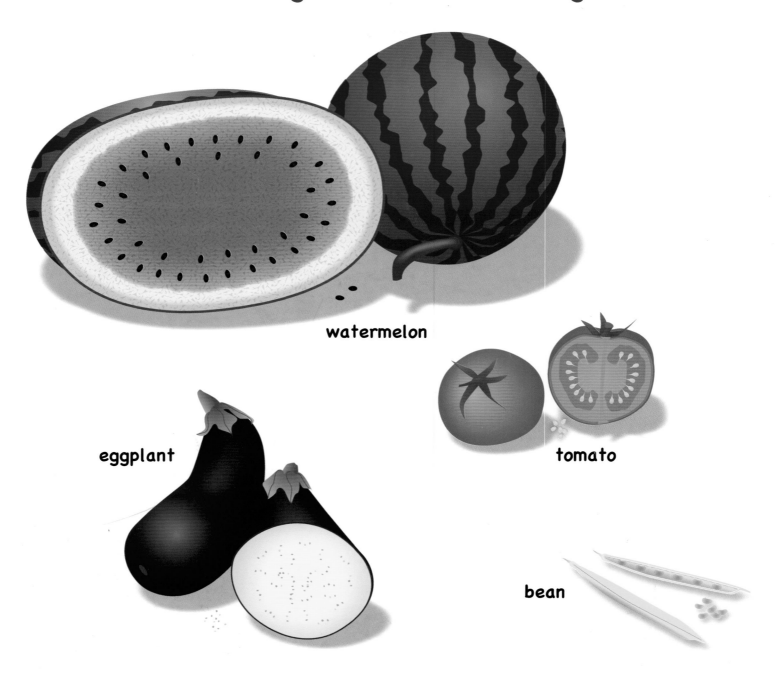

watermelon

eggplant

tomato

bean

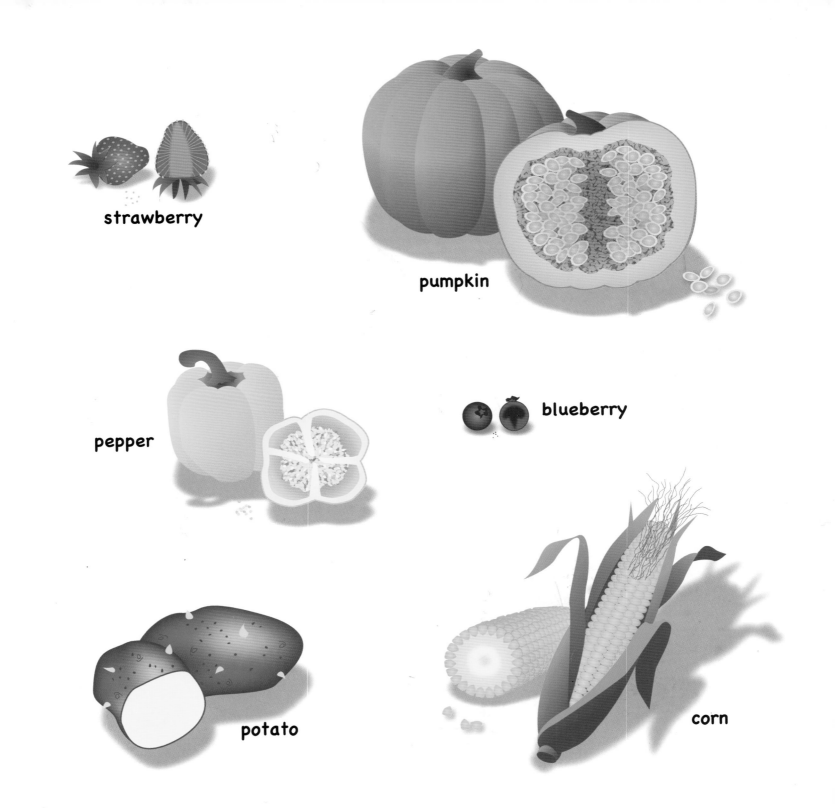

strawberry

pumpkin

pepper

blueberry

potato

corn

Can you find any of these creatures in the garden?

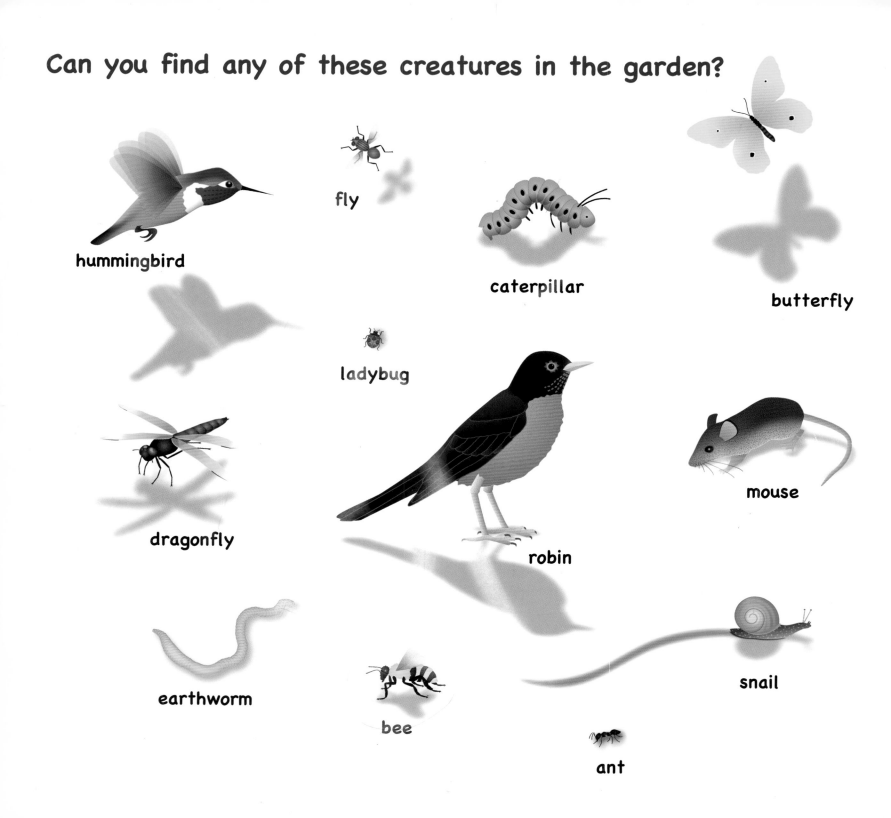

hummingbird

fly

caterpillar

butterfly

ladybug

dragonfly

robin

mouse

earthworm

bee

snail

ant